Who will be Louise's big buddy?

Louise gasped. She saw the looks of pity from her classmates. Sandra was the school's toughest bully.

"Poor Louise," said Becky sympathetically.

Sandra stomped down the aisle. Closer and closer she came. Finally, she stopped in front of Louise. Louise looked up . . . and up. Sandra seemed six feet tall.

Sandra turned a chair around and swung her leg over the seat, cowgirl style.

"Now you can spend a few minutes getting acquainted," said Mr. Shelby.

Louise
the One and Only

by Elizabeth Koehler-Pentacoff
illustrated by R. W. Alley

This edition published in 2002.

Published by Little Rainbow,
an imprint and trademark of Troll Communications L.L.C.

Printed in Canada.

10   9   8   7   6   5

Library of Congress Cataloging-in-Publication Data

Koehler-Pentacoff, Elizabeth
Louise the one and only / by Elizabeth Koehler-Pentacoff;
illustrated by R. W. Alley.
p.   cm.
Summary: Louise loves some of her kindergarten activities, such as painting, while from other school experiences she learns to give and take with her classmates.
ISBN 0-8167-3756-8 (lib.)   ISBN 0-8167-3757-6 (pbk.)
[1. Kindergarten—Fiction.   2. Schools—Fiction.]
I. Alley, R. W., ill.   II. Title.
PZ7.K81775Lo   1996   [E]—dc20   95-19112

Table of Contents

Chapter 1

I'm Not Louise

"Louise," called Mr. Shelby, the teacher. "Put away your art materials, please."

All of the other children sat at their tables with their hands folded. But not Louise. She cut out a big red heart and glued it to her paper. Next she used a purple crayon to draw a kite.

"Louise," said the teacher.

Becky's charm bracelet jingled. "Louise is going to get in trouble," she said in a singsong voice.

Richard, Louise's partner, poked her with his elbow. "You have to clean up now!" he whispered loudly into her ear.

Louise looked up to see the whole class waiting for her. She saw Mr. Shelby frowning. She

looked at Richard. Then she said, "But I'm not Louise."

"What?" asked Richard.

"Today I'm Charlotte," she said.

For a minute, no one did anything.

Then Mr. Shelby said, "Okay, Charlotte. It's time to put away your work."

Charlotte put away the scissors, crayons, paste, and picture into her cubby. Then she folded her hands like the other kindergartners.

The next day, everyone sat in a circle as Mr. Shelby called attendance.

"Becky."

"Here."

"Johnny."

"Here."

"Louise."

Mr. Shelby looked up from the list to see Louise looking out the window.

"Louise . . . I mean Charlotte," called the teacher.

There was no answer.

Richard yanked at Louise's shirtsleeve. "Say 'here.'"

Louise blinked. "I'm not Louise. And I'm not Charlotte."

"Who are you today?" asked Mr. Shelby politely.

"I'm Natasha."

"Natasha," said the teacher.

"Here," said Natasha.

When it was time for recess, Mr. Shelby said, "You may have the ball, Natasha."

"Thank you," said Natasha. She took the ball and ran outside to play.

"Richard, would you like the jump rope?" asked Mr. Shelby.

Richard put on his jacket but didn't answer.

Becky tapped Richard on the shoulder.

Richard said loudly, "I'm not Richard."

"Who are you?" asked Becky.

"I'm Sam."

"Sam, would you like the jump rope?" asked the teacher.

"Thanks," said Sam, running out the door.

By the time recess was over, Becky was Jessica, Brittany was Beth, Justin was Ryan and Keith was Steven. It was hard for Mr. Shelby to pass back papers. No one answered to his or her real name, and the teacher got all the new names mixed up.

But the next morning, Louise/Charlotte/Natasha, now Ingrid, greeted her teacher when she walked into the classroom.

"Hi, Mr. Shelby," she said. "Do you like my new lunch box?"

Mr. Shelby wrote the word "sun" on the chalkboard.

Louise/Charlotte/Natasha/Ingrid cleared her throat. "I said, do you like my new lunch box?"

Mr. Shelby drew a picture of the sun next to the word.

Richard/Sam, now Robert, pushed a truck across the floor. "That's not Mr. Shelby," he said, grinning. "Today his name is Mr. Green."

Chapter 2

Everyone Except Louise

"Who lost a tooth this week?" asked Mr. Shelby.
Richard waved his hand high in the air.

Becky stuck her arm up straight.

"Look," said Charlie. He opened his mouth. "My top tooth wiggles." He showed them proudly. All the other children sitting on the rug gathered around Charlie to take a good look.

"Well, Charlie, it looks like that tooth will be out in a day or two," said Mr. Shelby. "And congratulations to Richard and Becky. You're in our Lost Tooth Club." Mr. Shelby took his bright red marker and drew a picture of a smiling tooth next to Richard's and Becky's names on the chart.

Now everyone in the class had a happy tooth next to his or her name.

Everyone, that is, except Louise.

After school that day, Louise stared at her teeth in the mirror. She practiced wiggling them one by one to see if any of them moved.

They didn't.

Perhaps if she wiggled just one tooth, it would come loose.

So every morning before breakfast, Louise would wiggle her top tooth.

In school, when no one was watching, Louise would wiggle it with her finger.

And every night in bed, she would try to move it with her tongue.

One day at the breakfast table, Louise worked overtime on her tooth. Her brother, Martin, watched her. "What are you doing?" he asked.

"Wggggshimymooth," Louise mumbled. It was hard to talk with her fingers in her mouth.

"What's the matter?" asked her mother, looking above her newspaper.

Louise stopped long enough to explain. "I'm wiggling my front tooth."

"Is it loose?" asked her father.

"Not yet," she replied.

"Don't worry, Louise," said her mother. "I didn't lose any of my teeth until I was seven years old."

Martin smiled a toothless grin. "Me, too."

"Seven years old?" asked Louise. "But I want to lose one *now*!"

After breakfast, Louise and Martin walked to school.

"So you really, really want to lose a tooth right away?" Martin lisped.

Louise sighed. "Yes. Everyone else in my class has lost a tooth except me."

Her brother smiled. "I have an idea that just might work. We'll try it this afternoon."

Louise could hardly wait. When Mr. Shelby read a book to the class on animals, Louise studied the pictures to see if the animals had lost any teeth.

During art, Louise painted a large picture of herself . . . missing a tooth.

At recess she counted all the kids who had missing teeth on the playground.

Finally, it was time to go home.

When they got home, Martin went into the bathroom for a piece of dental floss.

"I'll tie one end of this string to a doorknob and one end to your tooth," he explained.

The doorknob part worked fine, but the floss was too slippery and Louise's tooth was too tiny.

"Hmm," mused Martin, studying Louise's mouth.

Louise swallowed. "Now what?"

Martin snapped his fingers. "I know. It worked for me!"

She followed Martin into the kitchen. Surely if Martin could get his tooth out, he could pull hers out, too.

He grabbed an apple from the basket on the table. "Here. Eat this."

"What?" asked Louise.

"Bite into the apple with your front teeth first. Apples are crunchy, so it will loosen your tooth," Martin said confidently.

Louise looked doubtful.

"Remember," he added, "it worked for me."

That afternoon Louise ate four apples. For breakfast the next day, she had three more.

"Why, Louise," exclaimed her mother. "I didn't know you loved apples so much."

Louise put down her last apple core. She didn't love apples anymore. She tried to wiggle her tooth. It still didn't move.

Martin scratched his head. "I can't understand it. I thought it would work."

"That's okay," said Louise with a small burp. "It was worth a try."

That week Mr. Shelby colored in three more teeth on the chart.

Charlie grinned, showing a gap in his front teeth.

"It's my *fourth* lost tooth," he bragged.

Louise stared at a grape juice stain on the rug.

Then Mr. Shelby put down his bright red marker. He cleared his throat.

"Today we also have a special award."

Everyone whispered and squirmed.

A special award? wondered Louise. *Charlie will probably get it for losing the most teeth.*

Mr. Shelby held up the most beautiful certificate Louise had ever seen. Around the border were colored flowers. In the middle was a beautiful smiling tooth.

"This is for the president of our Lost Tooth Club," he said.

"The president?" asked Becky, sitting up straight. "What does the president do?"

"The president will take over my duties for drawing teeth on the Lost Tooth chart," explained Mr. Shelby.

Charlie smiled. "I bet that's me," he whispered to Louise.

She bet it was Charlie, too.

"And this award goes to . . ." Mr. Shelby paused suspensefully.

"Louise!" Mr. Shelby finished. Everyone turned to look at Louise. Then Mr. Shelby handed her the award and everyone clapped. "Louise is the lucky girl who has kept her teeth the longest," said Mr. Shelby.

"Oooh," said Becky, examining the award. "You're so lucky, Louise."

"Wow," said Charlie. "You get to be president."

"Thank you, Mr. Shelby," said Louise, remembering her manners.

Mr. Shelby handed her his bright red marker.

She stood up straight and proud in front of the class. "Did anyone else lose a tooth today?" she asked.

Chapter 3

April Fools, Louise!

"Hey, Louise," called Richard from down the hall. "Your shoe's untied."

Louise bent down to tie her shoe. But she was wearing loafers.

"Ha, ha," laughed Richard. "April fools!"

Louise stood up. She could feel her face turning red. But it was okay. She'd pull a joke on Richard later.

Louise walked into the classroom.

"Good morning, Louise," said Mr. Shelby. "Did you bring your sleeping bag?"

"Sleeping bag?" asked Louise.

Mr. Shelby grinned. "April fools!"

During art, Becky passed the glue to Louise. "Oh no," cried Becky, staring at Louise's shirt.

"You have paint all over your elbow."

Louise sighed. It wouldn't be the first time. Last week when they did sponge painting, the sponge had landed right in her lap. And the week before that they tie-dyed T-shirts. Only Louise accidentally tie-dyed part of the blouse she was wearing.

Louise examined each elbow. "Where's the paint?" she asked.

"April fools," said Becky.

Everyone around them laughed.

Louise smiled at the joke. And she smiled with relief that she hadn't ruined her shirt. Okay, she thought. Now it was *her* turn to play a joke on someone.

On the playground, Louise yelled to Richard, "Look out for the ball!"

"What?" he asked.

"Look out for the ball," she screamed.

But Richard still hadn't heard. He ran over to her. "What did you say?" he asked.

Louise sighed. "Never mind," she said.

In the room, the class had free time. Mr. Shelby put stickers on everyone's printing homework.

"Mr. Shelby," grinned Louise. "Your shoe's untied."

He looked down at his feet. "Why, so it is.

Thank, you, Louise." He stooped to tie it.

Louise examined his shoes. Why, one untied, after all. Never mind, she thought. couldn't play a joke on Richard or Mr. Shelby, but Becky would be easy.

She walked over to Becky. She was sweeping out the playhouse.

"Becky," said Louise. "You have a rip in your tights."

Becky continued to sweep. "I'm not wearing any tights today." She looked up at Louise. "But I see that you have a rip in *your* tights."

"Sure," said Louise sarcastically, refusing to look down and check.

It was certainly hard to play jokes on people, she thought. She walked behind the bookcase and out of Becky's view. She peeked down at her legs. It was true! She *did* have a rip—right down her left knee!

"Louise," Mr. Shelby called, holding up a piece of paper. "You forgot to put your name on your homework."

Louise was about to claim her paper, when she stopped. She wouldn't be tricked again.

"How do you know it's mine if my name's not on it?" she asked suspiciously.

"I recognize the way you dot your *i*'s," he replied.

put my name on my paper," said
be someone else's."

shrugged and dropped the page
asket, where all unclaimed work

pin papers up on the bulletin
board.

Casually, Louise walked over to the
wastebasket. After first making sure Mr. Shelby's
back was to her, she peered inside.

Sure enough, there was her homework page,
with the *i*'s made with big black dots on top. Becky
made her *i*'s with the dots in the shape of hearts.

Quickly, she grabbed the paper and printed her
name on top. She placed it on Mr. Shelby's desk.

"Louise," said Richard. "You get to come
home with me today."

"No, I don't," said Louise. "My mom never
told me that."

"I know," said Richard. "My mom is going to
call your mom this morning."

"Sure," said Louise, not believing a word of
it. "You're just pulling another April fools on me."

Richard shook his head. "No, I'm not,
Louise—honest."

Mr. Shelby's phone rang. He answered it.
After a short conversation, he hung up and turned
to the class.

"Louise," he said. "Your mother has called the office. You can go home with Richard when his mother picks him up today."

Louise looked at Richard.

"See?" he said. "I told you."

Jokes sure can be confusing, thought Louise.

Everyone sat down at their desks to practice printing the letter *y*. Louise had fun putting smiling faces on hers. She hoped Becky didn't think of doing that.

Mr. Shelby worked at his desk. He bent down to straighten papers in the bottom drawer.

The classroom door opened and in walked the principal, Ms. Humphrey.

"Where's Mr. Shelby?" asked Ms. Humphrey.

Now was Louise's chance. "He's not here," she said loudly.

Mr. Shelby stopped organizing papers and crouched down behind the desk.

The class was so quiet that Louise could hear herself breathe.

"Well," said Ms. Humphrey. "I'll look for him down the hall."

As soon as she stepped out of the door, Mr. Shelby stood up, smiling. The class clapped and howled.

"All right," said Richard.

"Yoweee!" yelled Griffin.

"We fooled her!" exclaimed Becky.

"Good joke, Louise," said Mr. Shelby.

Suddenly the door opened. Ms. Humphrey peered into the room.

"April fools!" said Mr. Shelby.

"April fools!" shouted Louise and the class.

Ms. Humphrey laughed.

"Why did you want to see me?" asked Mr. Shelby.

"There's an elephant in your car," she said.

"April fools!" everyone shouted. Louise shouted the loudest of them all.

Chapter 4

It's Your Turn, Louise

Louise squirmed in her seat and waved her hand high in the air.

"Michael," Mr. Shelby said. "Would you like to be weatherperson today?"

Michael beamed. "Yes." He jumped out of his seat and walked quickly to the front of the room.

Louise lowered her hand. It wasn't so bad. She didn't get picked for weatherperson, but she still could be calendar helper.

Michael turned the pointer on the weather chart to the sun.

"Today is sunny," he said.

"Thank you, Michael," said Mr. Shelby.

Michael went back to his seat.

"And who would like to be my calendar helper

today?" asked Mr. Shelby.

Twenty-three hands flew into the air again.

Louise's heart pounded. Would Mr. Shelby pick her?

"Becky," said the teacher.

Louise traced the crack in her desk with her finger. She looked up as Becky swished by. Only Becky could swish.

Becky pointed her finger at the calendar. She was wearing a red sparkly ring.

"Today is Monday the seventh. Tomorrow is Tuesday. Yesterday was Sunday."

"Very good, Becky."

Becky smiled and her ring gleamed. She swished back to her desk.

"Time for painting," announced Mr. Shelby. Louise couldn't wait. She loved painting more than anything else.

Mr. Shelby gave directions. "The Bluebirds and the Robins may go to an easel. Sparrows and Hummingbirds stay at your seats. You may work on printing."

Louise was a Sparrow. She sighed and looked longingly at the painters. Richard had already dipped his brush into the green. Becky was carefully putting on the smock to cover her dress. Griffin was stirring his red paint so it sloshed over the side of the container.

Louise slumped in her seat and kicked at her desk.

"What's the matter?" asked Mr. Shelby, passing out the paper.

"I wanted to paint," she pouted.

"Have patience, Louise. Your turn will come," he said.

First Louise printed the alphabet on the paper in capital letters. Then she printed it in lowercase letters. Next she drew raindrops all around the border. She stared at the clock. When would it be her turn?

She watched Mr. Shelby hang up the wet paintings with clothespins on strings across the room.

Finally, after what seemed like hours, Louise got her turn. She ran to the easel Becky had used, because it was the neatest. The floor around Richard's easel was covered with paint spots. Griffin's brushes had paint all over the handles.

And then she painted.

Soon Mr. Shelby said, "Bluebirds and Robins, you may water your plants. Sparrows and Hummingbirds, clean up your paint stations."

Louise put her paintbrush under the faucet. It wasn't fair. She wanted to water her marigold now.

Sure enough, even the Hummingbirds got to go before the Sparrows.

When would she ever get to have a turn first?

"Now it's story time," said Mr. Shelby, after everyone had returned to their seats. "Who wants to tell a story?"

Louise was so determined to be first, that her hand shot up high into the air before anyone else's. She never even thought about what story she would tell.

"Go ahead, Louise," Mr. Shelby said.

Louise smiled. She had finally made it. She stood by her chair. Everyone else would have to tell their story *after* she told hers.

"You may start your story now," said Mr. Shelby.

Story? Louise gulped. What could she say? She wasn't ready. She stammered. "Once . . . Once upon . . . a time . . ."

Pictures of Cinderella, Little Red Riding Hood, and Snow White flashed in her head. But not one new idea came into her mind.

"Would you like someone else to go first so you can think for a while?" suggested Mr. Shelby.

Louise looked down at Becky's hand waving high in the air, her red ring sparkling and gleaming. Becky wanted to be first, too.

Louise stood straighter. "No," she said, determined not to give away her turn. She had waited too long to be first.

She cleared her throat. "Once upon a time, there was a girl who always wanted to be first." She looked at Becky. Becky quickly dropped her waving arm.

Louise continued. "One day her teacher let her be first. And then she was happy." She looked at Mr. Shelby. "The End."

"Very good," said Mr. Shelby.

After school, Becky walked over to Louise. "How come you told a story about me?"

"About you?" asked Louise.

Richard bounced his ball over to them. "You changed it from a boy to a girl, didn't you?" he asked Louise.

Griffin zipped up his jacket. "I got to be first at the drinking fountain yesterday," he bragged.

Then Louise realized something. Everyone always wanted to be first.

Mr. Shelby locked up the classroom. He smiled at Louise. "If I hurry, maybe I'll be the first teacher at the coffee machine."

Louise walked slowly to the car pool. She knew if she got there last, she'd get the best seat by the window.

Chapter 5

Hold Your Breath, Louise

Louise dreaded Thursdays.

Her beginning swim class met every Thursday.

During the first class, everyone practiced blowing bubbles. Louise blew terrific bubbles.

After bubble blowing, everyone dunked their heads underwater.

Everyone but Louise.

Richard dunked his head. Griffin put his head underwater and held his breath for ten seconds. Even Becky did it.

But not Louise.

"I can't get my hair wet," she explained. "We're going out to dinner tonight."

"Why don't you get a swim cap like mine?"

asked Becky, touching the decorations on her cap.

The next class, Becky brought an extra swim cap for Louise.

"Thanks a lot," said Louise. But the way she said it showed she wasn't really thankful.

She tugged it on her head. "It's too tight," she said, quickly pulling it off. She gave it back to Becky. "Thanks anyway."

A week later, the teacher, Maria, took Louise aside.

"It's easy to put your head underwater," said Maria. "We'll both do it at the same time."

She held Louise's hand. "On the count of three, we'll dunk our heads just for a moment. Okay?"

Louise nodded.

"One," counted Maria.

Louise gulped.

"Two."

Louise shivered.

"Three."

Maria dunked her head. Louise dunked her chin.

Maria came up. Drops of water clung to her eyelashes. "Your hair isn't wet," said Maria.

"My chin is," said Louise.

"Okay, let's just put our faces in the water."

Maria counted to three. She dunked her face.

Louise counted to ten. Then she bravely touched the tip of her nose to the water.

"Good start, Louise," said Maria. "But our swim time is over. Next week we'll dunk our whole heads underwater."

Louise climbed out of the pool. She didn't have to come back for one week.

But the week passed quickly, and soon it was Thursday again.

By this time everyone in the class had mastered head dunking and had begun kicking. Everyone except Louise.

"Louise," whispered Maria. "It's time for you to put your head underwater."

Louise stared at Richard, Becky, and Griffin holding onto the edge of the pool and kicking.

"I'll practice kicking," she said. "I know I can do that."

So Louise kicked. She kicked until it was time to go home.

That night, Louise played cards with Martin.

"Go fish," said Martin.

Louise stared at a cookie crumb on the table. What would she do next Thursday? She knew she couldn't hold her breath underwater. Water would get up her nose, for sure.

"Louise!" yelled Martin. "Take your turn."

"Oh," said Louise.

For a minute, no one said anything.

"What's your problem?" asked Martin. "Are you sick or something?"

Louise put down her cards. She stared hard at the crumb so she wouldn't cry. "I'm afraid to put my head in the water."

Martin put down his cards, too. "I know what you mean. It took me three months before I dunked my head."

Louise looked up from the cookie crumb. "Really?"

Martin nodded.

"How did you . . ." Louise began.

"I practiced holding my breath a lot. And when I got good at it, I put my head underwater in the bathroom sink."

"The bathroom sink?" Louise asked.

"Yes," said Martin. "And when I got brave, I tried the kitchen sink and then the bathtub."

So Louise practiced. She held her breath while riding her bike. She held her breath during art. And she even held her breath as she watched her favorite TV program.

At first she could only count to three before she needed air. But soon she made it to ten. One time she even held her breath through one whole television commercial.

Then she practiced in the shower. Next she

tried the sink and the tub. At first she only got her face wet. Finally, she submerged her head.

On Thursday she was ready. While everyone practiced the front stroke, Maria took Louise aside.

"Okay, Louise. On the count of three, let's dunk our heads."

But Louise didn't wait for the number three. She dipped her nose, chin, face, and head underwater and stayed there.

When she came up, Maria's mouth was open wide in surprise.

"Good job, Louise," she said.

Richard had been watching. "All right, Louise!" he yelled.

Griffin and Rachel clapped. Becky smiled at her. Louise felt great.

During that swim class, Louise dunked her head, kicked her feet, and did the front stroke. And she even put them all together.

"I'm swimming!" she said.

"Time's up," called Maria.

Everyone got out of the pool. Louise reached for a towel and handed one to Richard.

"You were great, Louise," he said.

Louise smiled. "I can't wait for next Thursday!"

Chapter 6

Let's Have a Talent Show, Louise

"Class," said Mr. Shelby. "I have an exciting announcement."

Louise sat crosslegged on the carpet. "I bet we go on a field trip," she whispered to Richard.

Richard leaned over to Louise. "Or someone famous will come to our class."

Louise remembered when a witch came for Halloween and a Native American came for Thanksgiving.

"Our school will have a talent show," said Mr. Shelby.

Becky waved her hand high in the air. Her charm bracelet jingled.

"Ooooh," she cried. "Mr. Shelby! I know what I'm going to do."

"What?" he asked.

"I'll be a ballerina and dance," she said. "I've taken ballet lessons since I was two."

Richard said he'd perform a magic act.

Griffin would sing a song.

Louise thought and thought. What could she do? She never took dancing lessons. She didn't know any magic tricks. And when she sang at home, her brother covered his ears.

At recess Louise climbed on the monkey bars with Richard.

"What are you going to do for the talent show?" he asked her.

"I don't know yet," she said, flipping upside down.

They heard jingling and Louise saw Becky walk over to them.

"Louise, what are you doing for the talent show?" she asked.

Louise didn't answer. She was thinking. What could she do?

Becky smiled. "Poor Louise," she said loudly. "Louise doesn't have any talent."

Louise stared at Becky's painted red nails. She didn't know what to say. Maybe Becky was right.

"Yes, she does," said Richard. He jumped down from the bars and faced Becky.

"She's my 'sistant."

"She's your *what*?" asked Becky.

Louise just hung upside down. She stared at the ground. Mr. Shelby walked over to them.

"I think Richard means that Louise will be his assistant," said Mr. Shelby.

"Right," said Richard.

"Great," said Griffin.

"Louise knows magic?" asked Becky.

Louise pulled herself up on the bars and sat above Becky's head.

"Yes. Richard and I do all kinds of magic. We even saw people in half," she said menacingly to Becky.

Becky backed up. "I–I think I'll play hopscotch," she stammered, and ran around the corner.

"I'll look forward to your magic act," said Mr. Shelby to Richard and Louise. He smiled and walked to the classroom.

Griffin ran to the slide.

"Can I really be your helper?" asked Louise when they were alone.

"Sure," said Richard. "It will be fun."

So Louise and Richard practiced all week long. Finally, the day of the talent show arrived.

Becky came in a pink tutu. Her skirt was covered with sparkles. It glittered when she walked. Mr. Shelby played "Moonlight Sonata" on the piano, while Becky danced across the stage.

Everyone clapped politely.

Griffin sang "Yankee Doodle" very loudly. But no one covered their ears.

Finally, it was time for the magic act.

For the first trick, Richard pulled a bouquet of flowers out of his hat.

"Wow!" everybody exclaimed. The audience applauded.

Next Louise locked chains on his hands. In only a minute, he escaped them.

For their third trick, Richard held up an empty cake pan and placed a cover on top. He tapped it with his magic wand.

"Abracadabra!" he said.

He lifted the lid to peek inside. Louise could tell from Richard's face that something was wrong.

"It didn't work!" he whispered to her. For an embarrassing moment that seemed to last forever, they just stood there. He couldn't lift the top off because then everyone would see the empty pan. Louise wondered what she should do.

People started whispering in the audience.

"I bet they'll mess up," said Becky loudly from the front row.

Then Louise had an idea. She pulled out a large red scarf from behind the magic stand. Slowly she waved it back and forth, as she had seen Richard do during rehearsals.

"We will use a magic scarf!" she announced.

Next she held the scarf in front of Richard's cake pan.

She bent down behind the scarf. "Is it ready yet?" she whispered.

Richard adjusted the cake pan behind the scarf. "Okay, it works now," he whispered back to her.

"Abracadabra," said Louise as she pulled the scarf away.

Richard lifted the lid of the pan. There was a delicious frosted cake!

"Ooh," gasped the audience. Everyone clapped.

Louise took the scarf, wound it in a ball, and shook it out. It was no longer a red scarf, but a blue one!

The audience clapped some more. Louise beamed.

Richard took a bow. Louise bowed, too.

After the show, kids crowded around them.

"Gee, you were the best ever," said Rachel.

Becky frowned. "Next year I'll learn magic for the talent show," she said.

"Next year we'll saw someone in half," said Louise.

Chapter 7

You're the Best, Louise

Louise stared at the bulletin board, trying to find her picture of the rainbow.

There it was, right next to Richard's picture. He had drawn a big city, complete with vehicles, buildings, and people.

She sighed. Next to Richard's fancy drawing, her picture looked so plain.

Louise walked back to her desk. She picked up a crayon. This time, she'd draw the best picture of all.

"Hey, Richard," said Rachel. "What are you making?"

Richard bent a piece of paper and taped it together to form a box. Next he cut out a rectangle. "I'm making a three-dimensional train," he said.

The children crowded around his desk to see. Louise joined them. She didn't want to miss anything. In only a matter of minutes, Richard had made the engine, complete with wheels and smokestack.

"Wow," said Rachel, picking it up. "Three dimensional!"

Everyone oohed and aahed at Richard's creation.

Louise cleared her throat. "I made a seven-dimensional train at home."

But no one paid any attention to Louise. Everyone was too excited about the train that could stand by itself.

Mr. Shelby patted Richard on the shoulder. "Good job," he said. "You're quite an artist."

"You're the best!" said Griffin. Everyone agreed.

Louise didn't say anything. She walked back to her desk and picked up her crayon. Richard's art was always better than hers. Why couldn't she be the best?

During recess, everyone ran races between the hopscotch squares and the jungle gym.

"The first one to touch the bars wins," yelled Richard.

Louise put her toes behind the hopscotch line and stared at the monkey bars. She wanted to be first. If she couldn't be the best artist, she would be the best runner.

Richard was the judge. "Get ready," he shouted. "Get set."

Everyone leaned forward over the line.

"Go!"

Louise ran into the wind and felt her shoelaces slap against her ankles. She glanced around her. She and Griffin were in the lead.

But just as she raised her arm to reach for the bars, Griffin beat her to it.

"Yippee!" he said, jumping up and down. "I won!"

"You're the best runner," said Richard.

"He just has long arms," grumbled Louise.

For snack time, Becky brought chocolate chip cookies. "I made them with my mother," she said, handing the first one to Mr. Shelby.

He bit into the cookie. "Mmm," he said. "These are delicious. Becky, you are the best cook!"

Louise accepted a cookie. "Thank you," she managed to say. But she didn't look at Becky when she said it. She was too busy studying the cookie. Were those flakes of chocolate in her cookie, or merely specks of dirt? Just to make sure, she brushed the cookie off with the palm of her hand. The specks were still there.

She might as well try it. Louise took a small bite as she watched Becky proudly hand out her cookies to the class. Hmm. It was good. She gobbled the rest of the cookie and wiped her mouth on the back of her sleeve. Yes, it was a good cookie. But not *that* good.

Louise thought of the time she tried to help her father barbecue hamburgers and she dropped her hamburger into the burning coals. And the time she made biscuits with her mother and she sneezed into the batter. Her mother had insisted on throwing it all away and starting over. And this morning Louise tried to make her own toast. It set off their smoke alarm.

She sighed. If she wasn't the best artist, runner, or cook, what could she be best in? Maybe she'd have to show everyone how wonderful she really was.

During music, she sang the loudest. Maybe Mr. Shelby would notice her voice and say that she was the best singer.

He didn't.

Richard noticed, however.

He stuck his elbow into her ribs. "Louise," he said. "Don't sing so loud! I can't hear myself."

So she decided to be the best in motor skills. When it came time to throw bean bags, Louise threw hers so hard that it accidently landed in the trash can instead of in the clown's mouth.

She fell off the balance beam because she was trying to raise her legs higher than anyone else.

She wanted to be the fastest jumper, but she ended up tripping on the jump rope.

After motor skills, Louise sat down and put her head on her desk. Maybe, she thought sadly, she wasn't best at anything.

"Play time," announced Mr. Shelby.

Louise lifted her head up. Well, she'd have to figure out what to be best in later. Right now she might as well try to have some fun.

She ran to the play chest.

"Louise, can I play with you?" asked Richard.

"Sure," she said.

Rachel turned to Louise. "But you said I could be your buddy during playtime," she said. "You promised we'd play police."

Becky reached for the princess crown in the chest. "No, she can't. Louise and I are playing castle today."

"We can all play police and castle," said Louise, taking charge. "We can pretend the princess needs police to find her missing diamonds."

"All right!" shouted Richard as he grabbed a sword.

Rachel put on a police badge. "I get to solve the case," she said.

Becky adjusted her crown. "My diamonds," she said. "Where are my diamonds?"

Mr. Shelby walked over to the group. "Louise," he said. "You have the best imagination."

Louise, sword held majestically in front of her, smiled proudly. "Would you say that again—louder, please?"

"YOU HAVE THE BEST IMAGINATION, LOUISE," shouted Mr. Shelby.

Louise was sure that even the third grade class across the hall could hear him.

"Thank you," she said.

Chapter 8

Who's Your Big Buddy, Louise?

Louise wiggled in her seat. She had to go to the bathroom, but it was almost time for the big kids' recess.

Maybe if she hurried, she'd beat them to it. Louise raised her hand for permission. Becky raised hers, too.

Mr. Shelby gave them bathroom passes. "Hurry back," he said.

"Don't worry," said Becky. "We will."

They walked out of the classroom. Louise peered around the corner.

"Any big kids?" asked Becky.

"I don't see any," said Louise. She ventured out into the hallway. "Let's go!"

They ran to the bathroom together. They

stopped at the door.

"You first," said Becky, pushing Louise forward.

Louise put her ear to the door and listened. Then she opened it a crack and peeked. "It's safe," she whispered. "No big kids."

They ran in and used the toilets as fast as they could.

"Hurry," said Louise.

"My tights aren't straight," complained Becky, twisting them around.

They heard voices from the hall.

"The big kids are coming!" said Louise.

They ran out of the bathroom, just in time.

Later that day, Mr. Shelby announced, "I have a surprise for the class. Mrs. Wong is going to bring her third grade class to our room today. Everyone will get a big buddy."

"Big buddy?" asked Richard.

"You can draw pictures for them, play together at recess, and sit next to them at school assemblies," said Mr. Shelby.

Louise couldn't wait. It sounded like a big buddy would be lots of fun. Maybe she and her buddy would end up being best friends.

There was a knock at the door.

"That's Mrs. Wong's third grade," said Mr. Shelby. "You'll meet your big buddies now."

Becky's big buddy was Katie, the prettiest girl in Mrs. Wong's class. She handed Becky a perfume scented envelope with flowers on it. "We'll be friends forever and ever," she said to Becky.

Louise hoped her buddy would be someone exactly like Katie.

A boy named Alex was Richard's buddy. He was the pitcher for the school baseball team.

Griffin's new friend was Paki. He had just come from Africa, and he had toys, games, and lots of neat stuff to share.

Finally, Mr. Shelby read Louise's name from the list. "Louise, your big buddy is Sandra Sneedly."

Louise gasped. She saw the looks of pity from her classmates. Sandra was the school's toughest bully.

"Poor Louise," said Becky sympathetically.

Sandra stomped down the aisle. Closer and closer she came. Finally, she stopped in front of Louise. Louise looked up . . . and up. Sandra seemed six feet tall.

Sandra turned a chair around and swung her leg over the seat, cowgirl style.

"Now you can spend a few minutes getting acquainted," said Mr. Shelby.

Becky and Katie bent their heads together and whispered and giggled. Richard and Alex talked about baseball cards. Griffin learned all about Africa.

Louise glanced at Sandra. Sullen, Sandra sat with legs apart. She avoided Louise's eyes.

Louise sank down farther in her chair.

The bell rang for recess.

Sandra got up to leave. "Hmph," she grumbled. "Who wants to be with a baby like you?"

Out on the playground, Becky played house with Katie. Richard and Alex played baseball. Griffin and Paki ran races. Louise made castles in the sand until Sandra Sneedly walked by.

"Baby stuff," she muttered, kicking the sandcastles everywhere.

The next day the class drew pictures for their buddies. Louise worked hard on her picture of a rainbow. It had to be good, since Sandra and the other big third graders would see it.

That afternoon, Mr. Shelby handed out the pictures from the third graders.

Louise looked at her picture from Sandra. It was the most beautiful picture of a horse Louise had ever seen.

That day at recess, Louise built another sandcastle. She watched Sandra walk toward her. This time Sandra didn't call her a baby.

"I wish I could draw like you," said Louise softly.

Sandra looked down at Louise. Then she walked by. But she didn't kick Louise's castle.

The next day Louise painted a picture of a horse for Sandra. It was not as good as Sandra's, but it was Louise's best work. She handed it to Mrs. Wong before school. "Give this to Sandra, please," she said.

During art, Louise and Becky had to go to the bathroom again. But this time they didn't escape soon enough. The big kids came in just as Louise and Becky were washing their hands.

"Look at the babies," said one girl to another. "Let's give the babies a bath."

Louise and Becky huddled by a sink. The girl turned on the faucet and plugged part of it with her fingers. Water sprayed all over them.

At that moment, Sandra Sneedly walked in.

Louise shivered. Now they'd *really* get it.

Becky clung to Louise. "I'm wearing a new dress. It's dry clean only," she wailed.

"What 'cha doin?" Sandra asked the other big girls.

"Having fun with the babies," one of them answered.

"Who are you callin' a baby?" growled Sandra.

The girl quickly turned off the faucet. "Nobody," she mumbled, and ran out the door.

Sandra stared at Louise and Becky.

"Guess we better get back to class," said Louise.

Sandra grunted in return.

Louise helped Becky straighten her tights.

Then they walked slowly down the hall.

Chapter 9

Louise, the One and Only

"Louise," called her mother. "It's time for school."

Louise put on her left shoe. Then she put on her right one, just like she did every morning.

When she got to school, she walked around the big oak tree three times, just like she did every morning.

During free time, Louise decided to draw a picture. She took out the crayons and lined them up, one by one, on the top of her desk. She glanced over at Richard. He had dumped his crayons in a big pile and a few had fallen to the floor.

"My, Louise," said Mr. Shelby, looking down at her crayons. "You certainly are neat."

Louise smiled proudly. She was glad he could not see her bedroom, with the Legos, cars, and game pieces all mixed together on the floor under her bed.

"I always line my crayons up this way," she said.

For recess, Louise headed for the swings. Every day she liked to swing first, then play on the slide, and then finally end up on the monkey bars. But today the swings were already full. She frowned.

"What's wrong?" asked Mr. Shelby, stuffing his hands into his pockets.

"There aren't any swings left," Louise explained.

Mr. Shelby looked at the empty slide. "You could play on the slide."

Louise sighed. "I want to play on the swings first, just like I do every day."

Mr. Shelby raised his eyebrows. For a minute they both stood and stared at the noisy children on the swings. Finally, Mr. Shelby spoke.

"You know, Louise, you don't have to do everything the same way every day. It might get boring. You could try to be different."

Did Mr. Shelby think that she was boring? "I don't do everything the same way every day," she said, her chin jutting out defensively.

The next day Louise decided to be different. In the morning she put her right shoe on first, instead of her left.

She avoided the old oak tree, and walked backwards into her classroom. She bumped into Richard.

"What are you doing?" he asked.

"Being different," she said.

During reading time, she held her book upside down. When it came time for drawing, she left her crayons in the box instead of lining them up on her desk. When Mr. Shelby told everyone to print their names on their papers, she printed her name upside down.

On the playground, she made sure Mr. Shelby was watching. Instead of running to the swings, she ran to the slide. But Louise didn't climb up the ladder like everyone else; she climbed up the slide. Her tennis shoes squeaked on the smooth metal. Once Louise made it to the top, she backed down the slide and became an airplane, complete with a noisy engine.

"What's Louise doing?" Justin asked Richard.

Richard pumped his legs so that the swing sailed higher and higher into the air. "Being different," he shouted. The breeze carried his voice across the playground.

"Look," said Becky to Rachel. "Louise is being different."

"Different?" asked Rachel as she watched Louise flying in a circle around Mr. Shelby.

Richard slowed his swing by dragging his shoes into the sand. He jumped off and hopped on one foot to the monkey bars.

Justin got off his swing and pretended he was a dog chasing an imaginary cat.

Becky made believe she was a trapeze artist and walked along the hopscotch lines, while Rachel twirled cartwheels.

Louise stopped being an airplane and became the cat Justin was chasing.

All over the playground, children decided to be different. The first graders stopped playing tag and became monsters. The second graders forgot all about their ball game and became cars, trucks, and trains. The new sounds and activities drew the principal out of her office to see what was going on. She walked over to Mr. Shelby.

"What's with the kids today?" Ms. Humphrey asked.

Suddenly Mr. Shelby did a handstand. "We're being different," he said, looking up at Ms. Humphrey.

The bell rang, and the animals, monsters, and vehicles all barked, roared, and choo-chooed

their way to their classrooms.

Mr. Shelby jumped to his feet. "Chirp," he said to the principal as he flapped away.

Louise stopped lapping up the milk in the pretend saucer and headed back to the classroom. She looked around. Richard had become a buzzing bee. Justin was still a growling dog, and Becky was singing into an imaginary microphone.

Louise wondered when everyone would get back to normal. The clock said it was art time and she was anxious to start her drawing.

Mr. Shelby rang his bell, the signal for quiet. Louise breathed a sigh of relief.

"It's drawing time," he announced.

Richard dumped his crayons into a heap and started a picture of a bee. Louise took out her crayons and lined them up, one by one, on the top of her desk, just like she did every morning.